QUEEN KIA's

8-step Guide to Friendships

BY

ANIESHA JACKSON / Aniesha Jackson

ILLUSTRATED BY ANASTASIYA RUDYK

Kindness & Respect, Oh Yeah!

Karoy Legacy Publishing

To find more books or contact the author, visit
www.anieshajackson.com

Illustrated by Anastasiya Rudyk.

ISBN 978-1-7365308-0-1

This book is dedicated to every child who is kindhearted, smart,
and most importantly, their true amazing self.
You are the type of friend the world needs!

Hey, I'm Nykia!
But you shall call me...
Queen Kia,
the smartest,
most "wonderfullest"

K NOW - I t - A ll !

You see, I know everything
and I am here to help guide you.

I am 9 years old and I am an EXPERT at life.
Hey, did you just laugh? Well, excuse me!

Listen, if you want to survive in this crazy world,
you need to do what Queen Kia tells you.
Ok, that was a little rude!
What I meant to say is,
if you want your life to be a little easier,
you need to read my book
at least 1000 times!

This book is all about friendships.
I mean, **hello,** that is the title of my book!

Now listen to me,
everyone needs friends.
They make your life
so much better.

Friends are great for playing pretend, going on adventures, and cheering up your gloomy day. But the best part about friends is that they are perfect for playing pranks on your annoying big sister.

Don't you want friends like that?
I know you do!
Follow my 8-step guide and you'll
be a friendship guru.

Ready? Well, turn the page!

Step 1: Smile

Smile, for goodness sake!
No one wants to be around someone
who has a scowl, a growl, or an owl
on their face.

Having a smile
is sort of like an invitation.
It lets others know
you want to be friends.

What in the Entire WORld
is on your face?!

Step 2: Say something

I know it may be a little scary
to talk to someone you don't know,
but if you want to make friends
you have to open your mouth and talk.

Talk about what?
About your favorite show,
a cool place you like to go,
the icky bug you saw
squished on the sidewalk
this morning, anything.
Say something!
Start with, "Hi!"

Step 3: Be yourself

Don't pretend to be someone you are not.
If you like spaghetti mixed with broccoli
or reading the dictionary to discover
new words, do so loudly and proudly!

Don't change who you are
just to have friends.
Be yourself.

Step 4: Be a friend

Share, care, help, listen, use polite words, laugh—
these are ways to make and keep friends.

Being a good friend gets you MORE friends.
What kind of friend are you?

Step 5: Find your kindness and respect crew

Everybody will not want to be your friend.
That is ok! Find the crew that is right for you.

Don't hang with kids
who tease others or
talk back to grown-ups.
Choose friends
who are kind,
respectful,
and like
you for you.

Step 6: Apologize

If you've done something wrong, say sorry.
Sometimes you hurt someone's feelings
and didn't mean to. Apologize.
Don't give a lazy "I'm sorry."
Instead, try saying this:

I apologize for _____.
I can see how that made you feel _____.
Please forgive me, I'm sorry.

Step 7: Know that friends come and go

A not-so-cute fact about friendships
is that you may lose friends.
You change, your friends change,
you move away, your friends move away...that's life!

Instead of getting sad about it,
read my guidebook AGAIN
and find another group of friends
who will accept and celebrate you.

Step 8: BE YOURSELF

Again? Yes, again! Be yourself.
You are crazy, creative, caring, courageous,
crabby (especially when you're hungry!),
curious, cute.

Alright, you get the point...
you are cool just as you are!
The world needs a friend just like you,
be yourself!

That's it guys!
Follow my guidebook through and through
and you'll become a friendship guru.
Until next time, Kindness and Respect, oh yeah!

Kind

Adventurous

Intelligent

Inspiring

Kooky

Amazing

Artistic

Knowledgeable

Imaginative

What makes you a good friend?
Write those traits on the lines
and then draw a picture of yourself.

Made in the USA
Middletown, DE
02 April 2022

63386105R00018